THIS BOOK BELONGS TO:

_____

TO READ WITH:

_____

For Sylvie and Oscar, and their mum and dad too – M.M.

PICTURE SQUIRRELS

Published in 2016 in Great Britain by Barrington Stoke Ltd
18 Walker Street, Edinburgh, EH3 7LP

www.picturesquirrels.co.uk

This story was first published in a different form in
Animal Stories for the Very Young (Kingfisher, 1994)

Text © 1994 Michael Morpurgo
Illustrations © 2016 Sam Usher

The moral right of Michael Morpurgo and Sam Usher to be identified as the author and illustrator of this work has been asserted in accordance with the Copyright, Designs and Patents Act, 1988

A CIP catalogue record for this book is available from the British Library upon request

ISBN 978-1-78112-512-0

Printed in China by Leo

Michael Morpurgo & Sam Usher

WE ARE NOT FROGS!

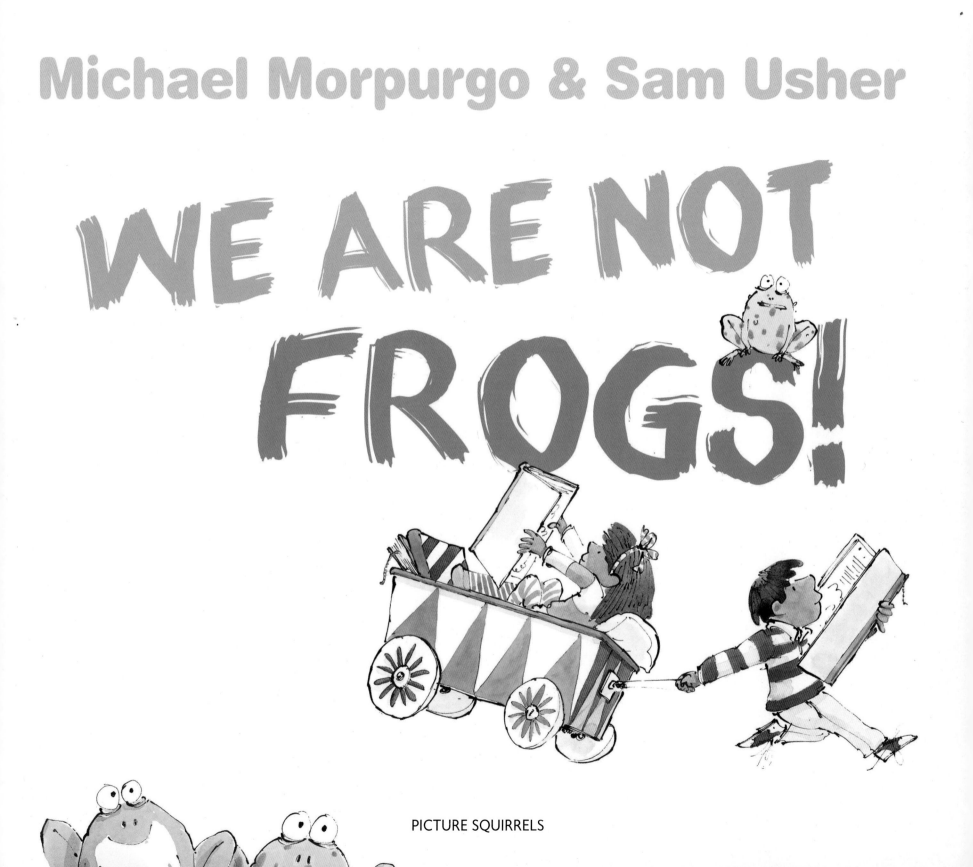

PICTURE SQUIRRELS

The storm was over and all the frogs and toads came hopping out onto the lawn to play long-jump. The frogs always chose long-jump because frogs can jump further than toads. And, of course, the frogs always won. The toads didn't mind all that much.

'Anything for a quiet life,' the toads thought.

All of a sudden, the door of the house opened. Mutt, a shaggy sort of sheepdog, came bounding out to bark at a lorry that was coming up the road.

Can you count 1 squirrel?

The frogs scattered into the safety of the flowerbeds under the porch and hid. The toads could not move so fast. So, instead, they stayed very still where they were and just hoped they would not be trodden on, nor eaten.

They were in luck. Mutt went roaring after the lorry, chasing it all the way along the fence until he was quite sure it would never come back. Then, with his tail high, and wagging with pride, he walked over to the porch and lay down in the shade. Soon he was fast asleep, his head on his paws.

It wasn't long after this that two children came wandering out onto the lawn. Jago was pulling a small cart. Alice was sitting inside the cart, and both of them were reading. They were taking turns pulling, but it always seemed to be Jago's turn.

'Anything for a quiet life,' he thought.

The toads were sitting in the long grass and did not see them coming till it was too late. There was only time to shout.

"Watch out! Watch out!" the chief toad croaked. He was the chief because he was the biggest and he had the loudest voice.

But Jago and Alice heard nothing.

They were far too busy reading.

Can you count 2 children?

It was very lucky for the toads that Alice finished her book just at that moment. She looked up and saw them.

"Look," she said. "Frogs!"

"We're NOT frogs," the chief toad croaked. He was quite annoyed, but no one heard him.

Alice and Jago kneeled down in the grass and caught them one by one in cupped hands with great care and put them in an ice-cream carton. Soon there were so many of them that they were all clambering on top of each other to get out.

"That's the lot," Alice cried, and she clapped her hands in glee. "We've got 14 frogs. Perfect."

"We're NOT frogs," the chief toad croaked, but the two children were now too busy talking to hear him.

Can you count 3 birds?

"They're all warty," Jago said, "and they feel dry and bumpy." And he poked one to make it jump. It didn't, so he tried another. "And they don't jump."

"All frogs jump," Alice said, and she peered into the carton.

Now the chief toad was really angry, and he croaked louder than he'd ever croaked before, at the top of his croaky voice. This time they heard him. This time they had to listen.

"How many times do I have to tell you that we're NOT frogs?" he croaked. "And will you please stop poking us? We are toads, and toads don't jump – not if we can help it anyway."

"Well," Alice said, "frogs aren't much fun if they don't jump."

Can you count
4 bees?

The chief toad thought as fast as he could. "I tell you what," he said. "You put us all back – with great care, mind – in our nice muddy ditch at the bottom of the garden, and I'll tell you where you can find real proper frogs that jump much much better than we ever could."

The children agreed right away and carried the toads down the garden to their muddy ditch where they emptied them out, but carefully, very carefully.

Can you count 5 butterflies?

"Thank you kindly," the chief toad croaked. "To tell you the truth, we wouldn't have been very happy in your house. We like it muddy, you see – all toads do."

"What about the frogs?" Alice said. She had no patience. "These jumping frogs. Where are they?"

"Over there," the chief toad croaked. "In the flowerbed by the steps. You can't miss them. They'll be jumping." And with a toady smile he sank into the mud and was gone.

Of course, the children found the frogs right where he'd told them. There were 22 of them. Alice counted them, and that was hard because they kept jumping all over the place.

Can you count 6 plant pots?

Catching them wasn't easy either, but at last they were all safe and sound in the carton, where they jumped up and down trying to get out.

Can you count 7 sunflowers?

"Good jumpers, these," Jago said.

"That's because they're frogs," said Alice. "But if they were kangaroos, they'd be even jumpier. I wish they were kangaroos!"

And just then Granny called out of the window. "Teatime. Chocolate cake!"

"Chocolate cake!" they cried. "Whoopee! Yummy, yum, yum!"

And they left behind the carton with the 22 frogs, and ran.

The frogs jumped and jumped, but the sides were too high and they just couldn't jump out, no matter how hard they tried.

Back on the porch, Mutt began to wake from a dream in which he was burying the bones of a very large lorry. A wasp walked along his nose and buzzed, so he woke up faster. He shook the wasp off and stood up and stretched and yawned. As he lifted his nose he smelled something he liked. It smelled to him a lot like chocolate cake. He licked his lips and padded across the lawn towards the kitchen.

Mutt was just passing the cart when he saw the carton – or rather he heard it. He looked inside. 'Jumping frogs,' he thought. 'Interesting.' He sniffed at the frogs and they jumped up at his nose. So he barked at them and then tried to touch them with his paw, but he knocked over the carton instead.

Can you count 8 ladybirds?

The frogs spilled out over the lawn. Away they went, jumping across the long grass in 22 different directions. Mutt could not make up his mind which one to chase, and so in the end he chased none of them. He was cross with himself, and so he chased the carton all over the lawn instead and pounced on it and chewed it and shook it.

Can you count 9 red flowers?

By then he was very pleased with himself. So he carried the carton into the kitchen to show everyone.

The moment the children saw the empty carton they burst into tears.

"Our frogs," they said. "Mutt's gone and eaten our jumping frogs!"

"They were our frogs," Alice cried. "We had 22 and now he's eaten them all."

"I won't ever talk to Mutt again," said Jago, and he pulled the carton out of Mutt's mouth and pushed him into his basket.

"Me too," said Alice. "We'll none of us ever speak to him again."

Can you count 10 plates?

And they both cried a lot more, and loudly too. But Granny was looking out of the window. "I think you'd better come and see," she said, and she pointed. "Over there by the flowerbed."

And when they looked they saw 22 happy frogs hopping away, all perfectly alive and uneaten.

"Well," said Granny. "Shall we have our chocolate cake now? And I think poor Mutt deserves a treat too, don't you? He doesn't look at all happy. Let's cheer him up, shall we?"

So they patted Mutt to cheer him up. But Mutt wanted something else, and they knew what it was. They gave him some chocolate cake. Then they sat down all together, and everyone had chocolate cake.

And the children smiled through the last of their tears, just like the summer sun coming out after the storm is over.

Can you count all 22 frogs?

Grow a love of reading

PICTURE SQUIRRELS